Moonlight
Through The
PINES

Tales from Georgia Evenings

JIMMY JACOBS

Published by
Franklin-Sarrett Publishers LLC
www.franklin-sarrett.com

Library of Congress Cataloging-in-Publication Data

Jacobs, Jimmy.
    Moonlight through the pines : tales of the Georgia evenings / Jimmy
Jacobs.
        p. cm.
    Summary: Presents a variety of wild episodes in the outdoors of Georgia,
involving truffle hunting, fishing, encounters with the marvelous hoop snake,
and other adventures.
        ISBN 0-9637477-3-8 (pbk.)
        [1. Country life-Georgia--Fiction. 2. Georgia--Fiction. 3. Humorous
stories.] I. Title.

PZ7.J152425 Mo 2000
[Fic]--dc21

                                                                00-028243

Illustrations by Cal Warlick
Author's Likeness by Zane Jacobs

Manufactured in the United States of America
10 9 8 7 6 5 4 3 2 1

Moonlight
Through The
PINES

Tales from Georgia Evenings

ALSO BY JIMMY JACOBS
TROUT FISHING IN NORTH GEORGIA
TROUT STREAMS OF SOUTHERN APPALACHIA
TAILWATER TROUT IN THE SOUTH
BASS FISHING IN GEORGIA

franklin•sarrett
PUBLISHERS

Table of Contents

When I was a boy growing up in the late 1950s and early 60s it was not uncommon for Southern youngsters, even ones living in cities, to spend a lot of time out in the woods sitting around campfires or whiling away winter evenings in front of log fires listening to their elders talk about the past. At that time, television was still new and had not taken control of our lives, nor claimed the total attention of young folks. Also, even though we lived in the suburbs of growing cities, almost everyone had parents or grandparents who had lived on farms or in small towns during the Great Depression of the 1930s. Many of the stories we heard dated back to events from that time.

Most of the tales that follow originated from the after-dinner talk and storytelling brought on by full stomachs, overstuffed easy chairs and long winter evenings. While other stories in this book have no direct relation to tales heard back then, the style of storytelling was greatly influenced by those winter evenings by the fire.

The characters in the stories are for the most part composites, and not meant to reflect any single member of the Jacobs clan, and admittedly, their escapades are often embellished a bit.

Do not bother to look for great truths about life in the pages that follow, since none were knowingly included. These stories are meant solely to entertain and if a few smiles are provoked then this book has been successful. And, in a small way, repayment will have been made to those who passed down the stories or tilled the fertile imagination of a young boy in preparation for inventing new tales.

Adventures Afield

Bocephus And The Truffle Hunt

The idea first came up during Wednesday night supper before prayer meeting at the New Sardis Baptist Church. Of course, that's how many things in life that you would rather forget have their beginnings. They start with an off-the-cuff remark and circumstances seem to snowball into wicked twists of fate that lead to inevitable results.

I was seated in my usual seat at the table nearest the ice tea refill pitchers. Buck Hartley and his family were at the table as well, leaving only two more places empty across from me. These empty seats attracted the attention of Mr. Thomas Alladay and his wife Maggie, who proceeded to join us.

Mr. Alladay was the new general manager of the Dixie Ridge Carpet Mill where I worked in the maintenance department. He and his wife had been transferred to the mill only three weeks earlier and were the subjects of much interest in town. Although her husband stood out here in Georgia because he was a New Jersey Yankee, his wife attracted even more interest since she was a very proper English lady, only recently arrived in our country, which she considered a "colonial backwater."

It was Mr. Alladay's desire to better understand his employees and ease his and his wife's entry into the community that brought the couple to the Baptist church on this evening.

After introducing the newcomers, we engaged in small talk as the meal began. As we ate, Buck and I fell into conversation about my latest unsuccessful turkey hunting venture from the previous Monday. Because much of the carpet mill's maintenance was done on Saturdays when the machinery was idle, my work week ran from Tuesday through Saturday, with Sunday and Monday as off days. It was a schedule which I enjoyed, since I still had a two-day weekend and on Mondays I had the surrounding woods and waters to myself.

As my tale of turkey hunting, to which Buck hung on every word and Mr. Alladay occasionally listened, wound down, we were surprised when Maggie Alladay spoke up.

"I was a bit of a huntress in my earlier years," she stated boldly in her very British accent.

The table was struck silent by her words, with no one, including her husband, seeming to have the slightest idea what to say next. Since this was my boss' wife, I felt responsible to rescue her from the uncomfortable silence.

"Is that a fact, ma'am," I said in an overly polite tone.

"Indeed, it is," she replied. "As a girl I rode to the hounds with my father and even did a spot of fowling with the men as well." Then as an after thought she added, "But I most enjoyed when we went afield hunting truffles."

Buck and I looked at each other wondering what in the world a truffle might be. Neither of us found an answer.

"Don't recall ever running into a critter called a truffle, ma'am," I offered hesitantly.

"Oh, I am sorry. It's not an animal, but rather it is a tuber - or more correctly a fungus. It grows near the roots of trees. I believe that oaks are where they are most often found," she stated with growing excitement showing in her speech. "They are known to exist here in America and the terrain of this region very closely resembles that of the estates where we hunted them in England. And, of course, they are quite delicious."

During her explanation, Thomas Alladay had gone to get a refill of tea. From his position behind this wife, he waved for me to join him. Excusing myself, I went over to him.

Looking a bit sheepish, Alladay began, "This is the

first real interest I've seen my wife show since we moved here. I would consider it a great personal favor if you would humor her and take her out truffle hunting."

My first reaction was to decline, seeing as how I had no earthly idea what the lady was talking about. But, on the other hand, it was the man who signed my paychecks that was asking the favor.

"I feel certain I could arrange either tomorrow or the next day off with pay, if you would take her hunting," Alladay added confidentially.

It was obvious to me that this man knew how to drive a hard bargain. It would be foolish for me to try to argue with his logic, so I decided to take the day off.

Back at the table I took a seat and turned to Maggie Alladay.

"If it's OK with your husband, Mrs. Alladay, I would appreciate it if you'd show me how to hunt these truffles one day real soon."

As both of us glanced over to her husband, Mr. Alladay nodded his bored approval of the scheme and went back to eating his dinner.

"That would be delightful," the lady beamed, "and the sooner the better. I do miss the thrill of being afield."

"How about Friday then?" I offered. "My Uncle Paul has several stands of good oaks on his farm and he wouldn't mind us using them. In fact, knowing him, he'll probably want to join us."

"Wonderful!" she exclaimed. "But do you suppose

we'll have trouble finding a pig?"

"A . . . pig?" I stammered. "I thought we were hunting truffles?"

"But we are. I knew many gentlemen who hunted truffles with hounds, but my father always thought them unfit. He fancied the use of a good boar to scent the truffles. Swine do have excellent noses, you know."

"You're saying we need a pig to smell these mushrooms for us?"

"Oh yes, we really must have one," Maggie Alladay replied.

"Well then, I guess we really are in luck. Uncle Paul has the prize boar of the whole county on his place."

We quickly ironed out the rest of the details of our planned hunt and agreed to meet at Uncle Paul's place on the following Friday morning. When I telephoned to tell him of our visit, he took the news in his usual quiet way.

"You mean to tell me you're bringing some fool foreigner out here on my farm to hunt toadstools with a hog?" he thundered. "I always knew the Good Lord ran short of common sense before he got to this family. Well, you can dang sure count on me going along. I wouldn't trust either one of you loose in the woods with one of my animals."

Uncle Paul is one of a dying breed of men who still believe that it is possible to make a living on a small family farm. It is his stubborn commitment to that idea that helped run off two wives, without ever having been blessed with any children. Now in the later years of his hermit-like life, he had found his farm animals to be at least as important as his relatives. For other folks he had very little use.

Due in part to his slender and wiry body, Uncle Paul was often told that he looked a lot like the country music singing legend, Hank Williams. It was a comparison he really liked to hear. When out in public, Uncle Paul always wore a cowboy hat like the ones Williams had on in the old publicity photos from the 1950s.

Thus, it was no great surprise when Uncle Paul named his prize 350-pound hog, Bocephus. That was the nickname Hank Williams had given his son, Hank, Jr., and since Uncle Paul had no son to use the name on, he gave it to the nearest thing to a son that he did have.

There was never a county fair that passed without Uncle Paul appearing in his cowboy hat, while he and Bocephus strolled about with matching red and white checked bandanas around their necks. It was also a yearly event for them to take home the blue ribbon in the swine division of the livestock contest at the fair.

"Now exactly what are you figuring on Bocephus doing?" Uncle Paul asked, obviously intent on protecting his prized porker.

"As I understand it, he'll smell these truffles growing underground around the roots of the oak trees and show us where they are so we can dig them up," I explained.

"And you say there are other hogs that can smell where these roots grow?"

"That's what they tell me, Uncle Paul."

"Then, by golly, Bocephus can do it too. There's not a better hog in the whole state. We'll be waiting for you Friday," the old farmer stated, ending our conversation.

Not really having any clear idea of what is considered proper clothes for a truffle hunt, I arrived at Uncle Paul's farm dressed in the camouflage I use when hunting turkeys. Figuring that truffles were probably not as skittish as an old gobbler, I did not bother to wear my face mask and gloves.

Uncle Paul and Bocephus both came out to meet me, the old farmer holding the end of a rope tied around the pig's neck for a leash. It was obvious that my uncle considered this something of a formal occasion since he and the pig had on their matching bandanas. Uncle Paul also wore his cowboy hat, with his usual overalls.

"I sure appreciate you helping me out on this, Uncle," I said as we shook hands.

"I durn near backed out," he replied. "Even went down the road to Sweeney's and tried to borrow his sow, so I wouldn't have to get Bocephus mixed up with a crazy foreigner. I'd have done it too, but she'd busted out of her pen and Sweeney hasn't found her yet."

At that moment we were interrupted by the sound of a car approaching up the long gravel driveway. Together we stood and watched the dark blue BMW draw near. From it stepped the final member of our hunting party. Maggie Alladay was dressed in knee-high black boots, tan jodhpurs, a red jacket and black riding helmet, as though she were headed to an English fox hunt. In her left hand she carried a riding crop. Uncle Paul stared at her in open-mouthed amazement.

"Will we be riding some good jumpers today?" she asked smiling.

"You have any horses?" I asked Uncle Paul in a whisper.

"All I got in the barn is a my mule Sarah and she hasn't jumped since she sat down on a rattlesnake," he replied, unable to take his eyes away from Maggie Alladay.

"Well, saddler her up," I muttered.

"Ain't got one," Uncle Paul said.

"What?" I snapped.

"I ain't got a saddle."

Mrs. Alladay received the news that her mount would be a full-blooded Cracker plow mule with the stiff upper lip that one would expect from a lady of breeding. She seemed less happy, however, about the fact she would be riding bareback and using a rope for reins.

Soon we were headed into the woods. Bocephus led the way, appearing to enjoy the chance to go for a stroll in the forest. Next in line was Uncle Paul, still holding the end of the pig's rope leash. Then came Mrs. Alladay astride the gray mule, holding the reins and whip in her left hand while her right had a death grip on the beast's stubby mane. Bringing up the rear, I eased along carrying a shovel over my shoulder.

Suddenly our pace quickened as Bocephus made a

beeline toward a thicket beneath some oaks.

"I believe he's scented one," Uncle Paul shouted over his shoulder. "I told you old Bocephus was a good one!"

Just then Sweeney's lost sow bolted from the thicket and headed home on the run. As Bocephus shifted into high gear he jerked Uncle Paul forward and began to drag him face down through the undergrowth in pursuit of the departing female pig. Sarah loped along after them at first, but when the pig dragged its owner through a yellow jacket nest, the insects rose to the attack just as the mule arrived. Very quickly the mule and rider joined the mad dash toward the Sweeney farm.

Realizing that I had no chance of overtaking them on foot, I ran back to Uncle Paul's house for my pick-up truck and headed for the neighboring farm by road. As I pulled into the barnyard it was alive with action.

The wire fences of the chicken coup had been leveled and hens were squawking and running everywhere. The lost sow lay flat on her stomach next to the pig sty with her legs spread in four directions, appearing to have knocked herself silly on the board fence while trying to get in on the run. Mrs. Alladay was also down nearby, flat of her back on the compost heap where Sarah had deposited her.

At the far side of the yard and fast disappearing were Sarah, Bocephus and Uncle Paul, while Mr. Sweeney stood in the midst of the commotion discharging a double-barreled load of rock salt from his shotgun at the backsides of the fleeing trio.

Once order was restored, I quickly explained to Mr. Sweeney that I was simply an innocent passerby who had stopped to offer assistance and would be glad to remove the lady from his manure pile. The offer was accepted and I laid her in the back of the truck for the ride to her house. I felt that Mrs. Alladay weathered the trip rather well, although she did mutter to herself a lot during the drive.

Oddly enough, Thomas Alladay never mentioned the incident to me. That is probably because he was afraid his wife would find out that he had set the hunt up. As for Maggie Alladay, she has never spoken to me again about anything and I suspect she even finds the sight of me to be upsetting. Fortunately, I won't have to see Uncle Paul again until the extended family gathers for Christmas dinner. Somehow though, I have a feeling that it will take much longer than that for him to forget or forgive me for introducing him to the exciting sport of truffle hunting.

Bodie And The Trout

As you get older, you realize more and more how much our lives are ruled by fate. Some folks might prefer to call it luck, but by any name it proves to be a major source of excitement in our everyday affairs. Spice is also added to our daily lives by the fact that we never know when these brushes with fate will occur.

I had stopped by the bait shop to pick up a few last minute fishing supplies before a weekend outing into the mountains. Since we would be backpacking into the Jacks River valley - far from the nearest road, let alone a store - a few extra trout lures in my pack seemed like a good investment and a wise precaution.

While I roamed the cluttered aisles, looking over

the dusty packages of catfish bait and bass lures in a rainbow of colors, fate laid her hand heavily on the door of the shop. Through the door walked Bodie Carter. If there is anyone in our town that fits the description of "fishing bum" more completely, I have yet to meet him.

Continuing my ambling amid the fishing tackle, only a few snatches of the conversation taking place between Bodie and Mr. Shaw, who owned the store, floated back to me. From what I heard, it was obvious that Bodie was retelling his latest tale of fishing success. It was also a reminder that Bodie was one of those individuals who had the gift for talking.

Here was a man who could sell instant freeze-dried water - all you needed to do was add water and shake. His sincerity could stretch the truth without ever reaching its breaking point. Any number of professions would have welcomed his ability to persuade people. Careers in used car or telephone sales come to mind immediately as perfect jobs with a need for his talents.

Fortunately, for the rest of us, Bodie had a higher calling. He never stooped to any work that would interfere with his fishing. It was his passion and what he spent most of his time doing. The rest of his waking hours seem to be spent telling the rest of us about his fishing.

Bodie and his wife had no children, owned a mobile home and lived off her pay checks from the poultry processing plant, plus some money Bodie occasionally won in local bass fishing tournaments. The way of life left him free to fish whenever and wherever the chance occurred. His only problem was finding partners with whom to fish. He had a way of ruining friendships in a hurry. If it wasn't his endless chattering that drove them away, it was the fact that he thought he knew everything about every subject that came up. His habit of borrowing a couple of dollars and forgetting to repay the debts, undoubtedly, also played a role in the situation.

At the front of the store I laid my selection of spinners on the counter, where Bodie eyed them.

"You must not be going after big fish," he observed. "You going to use those little things to catch some bream for catfish bait?"

"Nope," I countered, "heading up into the mountains to fish for trout on the Jacks River. Going to spend the weekend backpacking."

As the cash register rang, making a dent in my wallet, Bodie surprised me with his next comment.

"Never been trout fishing myself," he said. "Always thought about trying it, but just seemed too busy to get to it. Oh, I've caught some over the years while crappie fishing, but that was by accident. I mean I've never been out on a creek after them."

At this moment I suffered a flashback to my childhood when my mother would talk to me about the virtues of having good manners. It would, no doubt, come as a complete surprise to that sweet lady to discover that her words had ever scratched my rough boyish surface, but unfortunately, they had. Mama's teaching won out and I heard myself saying the next sentence as though it were someone else talking instead of me. I could not believe what I was saying!

"Why don't you come on and go with us?" I offered.

"What time are we leaving?"

"Tomorrow afternoon about 4 o'clock."

"I better get home and pack some stuff then," Bodie concluded as he headed for the door. After my new fishing companion had exited, Mr. Shaw spoke.

"You feeling all right," he asked, giving me a look of pity.

"I suppose so," I replied, "Why?"

"Just never heard anybody beat Bodie to the punch before. He's usually already invited himself to go fishing before anybody gets a chance to invite him on their own."

When Bodie Carter met us at the appointed time, he looked much like an Army surplus store in the process of moving. His camping gear was mostly old World War II items with a few pieces that looked like they might be even older. When he put on his backpack with all its bulges and sags, he looked like a man being swallowed by a huge olive green marshmallow.

Once on the trail, our offers to help carry some of his gear only met with scoffs and set Bodie talking about the only good camping gear being the solid old fashion type. Undoubtedly we would have been treated to one of his long speeches on the subject, but he was soon faced with the impossible task of trying to talk at the same time his tongue was hanging out from exhaustion.

Having given up on helping him, we simply tried to stay on the uphill side of Bodie to avoid being swept away in an avalanche of camping gear should he stumble. Soon, however, it was our turn to suffer from trying to keep up with him. As we went over the mountain top and began to descend into the river valley, Bodie gained more and more speed as he trudged downhill under the load. We looked like a platoon of British soldiers marching at quickstep by the time we reached the Jacks River.

We all agreed to douse our campfire early that evening and welcomed the chance to get into our tents to rest after the day's hike. It was soon a guessing game as to whether the noise coming from Bodie's sagging moth-eaten tent was snoring or moans of agony. We took his red and bleary eyes the next morning as a hint to the answer to that mystery.

After breakfast, we began putting our rods and reels together for a morning of casting in the clear mountain waters for rainbow trout. Since trout fishing is a sport that calls for sneaking up on the fish and delicate casts, the rest of us chose ultra light rigs for casting tiny spinning lures. Not so, Bodie. What we had taken to be his walking stick on the descent of the mountain turned out to be his fishing rod. It was a solid heavyweight model that would have been useful for shooting pool or beating off the attack of a pit bull. Of course, Bodie had a logical reason for his choice of such stout fishing equipment.

"You boys go ahead and catch some little ones for dinner. I'm going to see if there's any 'hawgs' in here." With that he disappeared upstream along the river trail.

I was the first of the group to get back into camp at lunch time and began cleaning the two rainbow trout I planned to fry for the noonday meal. Moments later Bodie appeared, but looking quite different from the way he had when he left camp. In fact, he had the look on his face of a whipped puppy, which went well with rest of his overall condition.

Bodie's pants and shirt were both in tatters, and he would probably have been covered with even more mud than he was, if he had not obviously taken a recent dunking in the river. He was drenched and dripping as he entered the camp. After some encouragement, he began telling the story behind his present condition.

"After I left camp this morning," he began, "I was walking along the trail at a place where it overlooked a couple of deep pools. I could see right down into that clear water even though I was a good 100 feet up the hillside. Didn't really expect to see anything, since I don't usually even bother to cast to water on the lake if I can see the bottom.

"Anyway, I saw this big old trout just finning in the current down there below me. I swear that fish would have topped 5 pounds. It was a big one," he said shaking his head. "I began to climb down the hillside real easy like, planning to slip up on the trout. I hadn't gone more than a few feet when I pulled back a bush limb and down there on a rock on the river bank I see this blonde, long-haired hiker lady. She was taking her clothes off to go swimming."

During this part of the story Bodie's face reddened a bit, but it was difficult to tell whether it was embarrassment over having stumbled onto the lady undressing or if it was anger over having his fishing hole disturbed.

"Being a gentleman, I decided to sort of sneak back up to the trail and go about my business, but when I tried to turn, my feet went out from under me and I went rolling down to the river through the most gosh awful briar patch I've ever seen. When I rolled out the bottom, I went right off a rock and into the pool."

"I guess that was pretty embarrassing for both of you," I agreed.

"Couldn't really say," Bodie replied thoughtfully. "When I came back to the surface I didn't see hide nor hair of the lady. Only thing I did see was her clothes on the rock and some ripples on the water that looked like maybe they were footprints she left behind when she ran across the top of the river."

"And the big old trout was gone," Bodie concluded, long-faced and dejected.

The Art of Eating Crow

Southerners tend to be a people who are proud of their language. For decades the way we have spoken has set us apart from most other Americans. When we open our mouths to speak, out come words not used elsewhere.

For some reason, Yankees seem to have trouble understanding a simple sentence like, 'Bring that chair over c'here and have a seat.' To the Southern ear, one is a thing to sit on and the other is a place to put the thing to sit on. Or try telling a Northerner that the nearest telephone is 'up yonder on the coner,' and he may fail to realize the intersection just up the street is 'yonder' or exactly what a 'coner' is.

It is sometimes thought that Southerners are born with the ability to speak this way. We do, however, have to learn the art. For instance, when my daughter Tiffany was about six years old, she once asked, "Where is summers?" Figuring that perhaps she was having trouble understanding the changing of the seasons, I tried to get more details. I ask her where she had heard about this place.

"Granddaddy said he's going summers this week-end," was her reply.

Thus we have positive proof that we are not born with the ability to turn English into Southernese. It takes our children a while to master the art.

Not all sons and daughters of the South speak alike. Folks from Texas do have a bit of a different sound. Of course, some would argue that Texans are not Southerners, but Westerners or Southwesterners. Texans themselves will deny being any of the three, however. They claim that since Texas is bigger than all three of those regions combined, it obviously can't be in any of them. It would have to be a big state just to hold all the supersized egos that Texans seem to have.

Probably the best example of Southerners with a special sound are the Cajuns of south Louisiana. Their unique speech pattern contains a mixture of English, French and Spanish, plus assorted African and Carib-bean words. Personally, I think they simply talk funny from having eaten too much of their red-hot and spicy Cajun food.

Some folks even say that Southerners have the

tendency to ramble and beat around the bush when they speak, which brings me back to the purpose of this essay. Our language in the South is full of colorful figures of speech. That is not all that unusual since these appear in all regions of the country. On the other hand, we Southerners have a way of taking them a bit more seriously at times.

For instance, there is the term, "eating crow." The phrase, of course, means reaching a point of regretting some earlier remark that has come back to haunt one. Had only it been that easy in my case, I would have been perfectly happy!

The September Saturday morning featured blue-bird-clear skies, with just enough of a cool breeze blowing to take the edge off the late summer heat.

Unfortunately, such weather also means the lawn continues to grow, so I found myself facing the prospect of a day of yard work.

At the time it seemed like a reprieve when my sons, Brent and Zane, burst from the house in an explosion of preteen energy. Their mission was to remind me that I had promised to take them hunting as soon as we had a free Saturday. Not wanting to prove to be an unfit parent, I quickly gave in to their demand and began rounding up gear for a morning hunt on the nearby Allatoona Wildlife Management Area.

Before the car was loaded the boys came back out to ask if a friend could go along on the hunt. Again, I agreed, but did say that I would have to talk to one of the friend's parents to make sure they understood this was a real hunting trip, complete with shotguns.

I soon found out that although I had been speaking of "friend" as singular, the word had been offered up by two sons, resulting in it becoming "friends" by the time I got to the phone. To my great surprise, both sets of neighbors were overjoyed to have their sons get to venture into the woods with a genuine outdoorsman as guide. Naturally, before we could get this expanding troop in motion, yet another neighborhood boy showed up, another phone call ensued and our number grew to one adult and five adolescent boys. While Brent, Zane and I were armed with shotguns, the other boys carried only air rifles.

Packed in the car and speeding northward for the great adventure, one of the huddled mass in the back seat finally asked what we would be hunting. I explained that the only seasons open this early in the year were for squirrels and crows.

"Crows?" came the retort from the back seat. "Who'd want to hunt a crow?"

I explained that crows were such a nuisance to farmers and gardeners, plus they multiplied so fast, that they needed to be thinned out.

"Of course, not many folks hunt them since they are not very tasty," I concluded with a laugh. "Anyway, we'll be hunting squirrels, because we only shoot things we intend to eat."

Suffice it to say, entering the forest in search of wily squirrels with five half-pint nimrods full of adolescent vigor will send all the bushy-tailed critters scurrying for the next county. Unlike city park squirrels, a wild one heads for cover when people enter its territory. Genghis Khan and his Mongel hordes could not have equaled the clamor we made as we swept through the woods.

After a couple of hours of this fun in now 80-degree temperatures, I was sweating under the load of a game bag full of empty cans the boys had picked up along the forest paths. These had been deposited on dirt banks and summarily blown full of holes with a load of 20-gauge bird shot. Well, at least each of the boys would have some form of trophy to take home from the hunt.

Now it was time for me to bring out my secret weapon to save the day and make the hunt a success. Gathering the boys around me on a point of land covered with hardwood trees and sticking out into Allatoona Lake, I pulled from my pocket a squirrel whistle. A squirrel whistle is one of those gizmos that are generally given to you by a brother-in-law or some other n'er-do-well. It is something that you leave laying around the garage until one day you become fool enough to actually try it out.

I told the boys to spread out in the bushes and I would blow the squirrel whistle. It would sound like a baby squirrel in distress and the other squirrels would run out on limbs to look for the unfortunate bushy-tailed tot. When they showed themselves, we would soon be on our way to collecting the ingredients for a titilatingly delicious squirrel stew.

After blowing the infernal whistle until I was blue in the face, I thought all I was going to get from the effort was the chance to show the boys what hyperventilation meant. But, to all of our surprise, a shadow came bee-lining across the lake straight for us. At least something was interested in the plight of a helpless squirrel tot.

The blue-black wings of a crow flapped rapidly as it headed for our position. The chance to pick off a helpless baby animal is one that no self-respecting crow would ever pass up. As it streaked overhead, still too high for an easy shot, I instinctively raised the shotgun and touched off our first shot of the day at game. Too my utter amazement and consternation, the birds wings crumpled and it plunged down, landing almost at my feet.

"Great shot, Dad!"

"Are you really going to eat that thing, Mr. Jacobs?"

The questions pounded me as I looked down at the scraggly scavenger at my feet.

"Can I carry it for you?"

Needless to say, the crow accompanied us through the rest of the day. When the troop re-invaded the home neighborhood, the bird made the rounds of all the boys' homes, where parents and anyone else who happened to be around were informed that Mr. Jacobs down the street was going to eat the thing.

A man of lesser principle would have managed to

make the bird disappear that night, then lied and claimed to have eaten it. Unfortunately, I did not think of that option at the time. Instead I cleaned the bird just as I would have a dove. The result was a very dark-colored chuck of breast meat that would probably have looked appetizing had I not known what it was, or if I could have managed to forget what cleaning a crow smelled like.

Having noted that television chefs always marinate their meat before cooking it, I figured such an action was bound to improve the taste of my crow. Looking in the refrigerator for something in which to marinate the fowl, all I found was a bottle of cranberry juice. It would have to do. I marinated the meat in the red liquid for 48 hours, then smeared it with butter, wrapped it in bacon, dusted it with flour and baked it for an hour.

When you ask a hunter or fisherman about the taste of some game or fish he has harvested, invariably, the reply is "just like chicken." Served with a few fresh vegetables, I can truly say that a crow does not taste anything like chicken. As I recall, it tasted much more like a crow that drowned in cranberry juice than anything else that comes to mind.

Which brings me back to the original topic of figures of speech. We Southerners do tend to take them a bit to literally. Next time, I suspect that if I end up with a crow in the game bag, I'll opt to "eat crow" and bury it somewhere in the woods, instead of taking it home to eat crow and further build my culinary legend in the neighborhood.

The Bushy Eyebrow

My grandfather used to mention from time to time that the three types of folks for which he had no use were fools, pharisees, and pettifoggers. Now before you turn the page in disgust and move on in search of more interesting reading, let me unequivocally state that in spite of mentioning those three types in the opening paragraph, this discussion is not about Yankees or lawyers. In fact, grandpa was always quick to point out that in the case of those two classes of people, ignorance and hypocrisy should not be looked upon as personality flaws but simply as inborn characteristics.

The reason these sage observations come to mind is because I recently took up the art, habit, or disease (you can pick your own appropriate descriptive term) of tying fishing flies. I'm sure that in some cozy corner of heaven my grand sire is kicked back in a straight-back, cane-bottom chair in front of a potbellied stove and shaking his head over the fact that his namesake grandson has fallen into one of his despised classifications. After all, only a fool would voluntarily become a fly tier.

Don't get me wrong. I have never felt that fly fishermen were particularly foolish. Rather, I have always opted for the word "odd" when describing them and have even counted myself among their number for a couple of decades. It's just that when fly anglers get the itch to start creating their own flies their innate bent toward foolishness becomes apparent.

The usual excuse for this behavior is that they find it relaxing as well as being a lot more economical than purchasing commercially tied flies. As you watch one of these converts seethe at his tying vise (or should it be spelled vice?), however, working himself into a hair pulling frenzy while destroying a small fortune in fur and feathers, you naturally develop doubts about those explanations. And, of course, as with most endeavors there are some unforeseen consequences with which one must also eventually come to grips.

In my own case, I suspect that my problems all originated in the fact that I was just too good at tying fishing flies. The realism I achieved was astounding and quickly led to complications. The best illustration of my dilemma can be seen in the history of a fly I developed called the "Bushy Eyebrow." The name of this concoction may seem out of place since the object of tying flies is to imitate some bug that a trout will find appetizing. The finished product should come close to looking like the particular insect in question and will usually be named after that bug. Thus we have flies like Elk-Hair Caddis and Black Gnat.

In this instance the rule holds as well. When I finish tying this trout morsel, it closely resembles the black, bushy and frighteningly ugly eyebrows of the elderly men who sat on park benches of the neighborhood where I grew up. Those gentlemen invariably possessed a single eyebrow that shaded both eyes and the bridge of their noses to boot. At any rate, one look at the completed fly and the name seems appropriate.

This description may seem to put the lie to my claim that my flies so closely resemble trout food that they have gotten me into several uncomfortable situations. Not so! When I approach the task of creating some flies, I will amass my feathers, string, hooks and assorted furs with the stated objective of tying some standard, mundane fly pattern produced by innumerable other craftsmen. Invariably, however, regardless of whether I start out to tie a Royal Wulff or a Light Cahill, the same phenomenon occurs every time.

Once I begin to wrap fur and feathers on a hook, a metamorphosis takes place. Try as I may to control it, this shape shifting soon turns the fly into a Bushy Eyebrow. As I have noted, this is obviously the result of my having been too lifelike in my work. There are many examples in the insect world of creatures that go through a similar metamorphosis as they change from pupa or nymphal stages into adult bugs. I can only assume that my lifelike imitations suffer through this same change.

For a while I did not recognize the truth about what was occurring and in many cases even went so far as to toss the finished product into the trash can. Indeed, I would probably be a happier man today had I continued to dispose of all these flies in that manner. Unfortunately, some of the Eyebrows found their way into my fly box and actually accompanied me on fishing outings.

My troubles began in earnest while I was on a fishing trip far up the headwaters of Jones Creek, deep in the Blue Ridge Mountains. Fishing on this particular stream is limited to the use of artificial lures only, and I had pounded the water with every pattern of fly with no success. Finally, in desperation, I reached for a Bushy Eyebrow that was cowering in the corner of the fly box.

No sooner did this mutation touch the water than a brown trout impaled itself on the hook hidden amid the tangled fur and feathers. To my amazement I began to catch fish on practically every cast; at times several trout would be vying for the honor of grabbing my offerings. Needless to say, I was even more astounded when a rather beefy hand grabbed me solidly by the shoulder from behind.

Turning I found myself face to face with a rather irritated game warden. It seems that I had wandered into the middle of a stake out operation. I was quickly apprised of my rights and informed that although the warden had not figured out my method, he was none-theless convinced that I was violating the law by using natural bait. He based this assumption on the fact that no one could possibly catch the number of trout he had watched me take on my Bushy Eyebrow without having actually been tipping the hook with a worm.

As usual in such a situation the warden began a thorough search of my fly vest and other gear for the offending natural bait. All the while I was assuring him that I had broken no laws or even breached any customs or ethical standards of the sport. When I showed him my Bushy Eyebrow, he snorted with laughter at the idea that it could possibly attract trout and then warned me not to trifle with his good nature.

In the end my protestations were to no avail, however, and the warden's failure to locate contraband led him to be even more thorough in his search. Finally unable to contain myself, I asked if strip searches were customarily performed at stream side and if they were, had he ever actually located any night crawlers in the boxer shorts of a poacher?

A general rule took shape in my mind that day and I have followed it religiously ever since. Fly tiers should never talk back to anyone charged with uphold-ing the laws of the state. As I sat dejectedly in the holding cell at the county jail, amid the snores of a gentleman sleeping off the previous evening's inebria-tion, I wondered how many other anglers had found themselves cited and locked up for blaspheming the game laws of Georgia?

Although quite disturbing at the time, my scrape with the game laws proved to be a boon from heaven. As a result of the ensuing publicity, word of the Bushy Eyebrow spread rapidly and my renown as a fly tier was soon earning a small fortune as I cranked out Eyebrows for sale as quickly as I could mangle the feathers.

The success led to my second and even more disturbing brush with the guardians of our lakes and streams, when I was summoned to the local district fisheries office. Upon reporting, I was informed that they wanted my cooperation in saving the trout population in the state. In point of fact, they wanted my assurance that I would not fight the ban they were about to announce on the use of the Bushy Eyebrow in the state's trout waters. Word had been filtering in for weeks that indicated anglers were using my flies to denude the creeks and rivers of fish.

Being a public-spirited individual, I agreed on the condition that they outlaw all other trout baits that were equally successful at putting fish in the frying pan. Quickly huddling, the state folks came to the conclusion that there would be too much political fallout if they banned the use of earthworms and nibblet corn for fish bait.

After some extended negotiating, a compromise was reached under which it would be a misdemeanor to fish with a Bushy Eyebrow on any public water where children or pregnant women were present. Noting that these folks were the most vulnerable in society, the state felt a responsibility to protect them from being scared witless upon seeing a Bushy Eyebrow come drifting down a creek toward them.

Recognizing their point, I agreed to the compromise. Also influencing my decision was the rather thinly veiled suggestion that was offered, hinting that if I did not agree the Fisheries Division would refer the matter to the Environmental Protection Division, which would undoubtedly regard the regular dunking of Bushy Eyebrows into state waters to be a type of toxic pollution. Once the partial ban was made public, the demand for the Eyebrows subsided and I soon gave up tying them. Of course, the taint on my character still remains. I was a fool to have ever tied the first one.

Since that adventure with the Bushy Eyebrow, I have resisted the temptation to take a dictionary in hand and look up the definition of pettifogger. Realizing that from time to time I have been a bit hypocritical like a pharisee, I find myself indicted on two of Grandpa's admonitions. If I looked up the meaning of pettifogger, I fear that I might run the risk of finding myself to be a three-time loser.

Cherokee Tales

It was a late February afternoon and the old sand road was drenched in unseasonably warm sunshine as I strolled through the woods with my sons, Brent and Zane. The "false" spring day, not an uncommon occurrence in the deep South, just begged for outdoor activity. The promise it held was for an end to the long cold months of winter's cabin fever.

"What's this, Dad?" Zane, the younger boy, asked, holding a piece of slick-surfaced rock he had picked up.

"Looks like an arrowhead," was my reply.

"Let me see," Brent said, peering down at it.

"What's it made of?"

"That's flint," I explained. "It's what the Cherokee

Indians used to make their arrow points."

As we moved on both boys took turns rubbing the slick sides of the arrowhead or running their fingers gingerly along the sharp, chipped edges of it.

"Were there Indians around here?" Zane asked.

"Duhh! How do you think the arrowhead got here?" Brent chided his brother.

"This part of Georgia to the north and west of the Chattahoochee River was part of the Cherokee Nation up until the 1830s," I jumped in to explain, hoping to cut short the brotherly argument that was brewing.

Although Zane managed to toss a "doofus" under his breath in Brent's direction, a small critter scurrying across the road caught their attention and short circuited the hostilities.

"What was that?" Brent asked.

"I didn't see it," I answered. "What did it look like?"

"It was little and red," Zane explained.

"Did it have stripes on its back?"

"I think so," Zane confirmed.

"Sounds like a chipmunk," I stated with appropriate fatherly assertiveness. "Of course, chipmunks didn't always have stripes on them."

"They didn't?" Brent said.

"Nope," I began again, "in fact, the Cherokees told a story around their campfires that explained how the stripes got there."

"Tell us about it," Zane pleaded, with a second from his brother.

The Cherokee Indians believed that everything had a spirit all its own. In the case of plants they thought the spirits were good and friendly to man. As a result, the Indians knew of more than 500 plants that they could use for food or medicines. On the other hand, the spirits of animals were thought to be unfriendly to man and carried diseases.

The reason the animals' spirits carried diseases went back to the time long ago when birds and animals could still talk. As a matter of fact, this was back when the critters lived in villages like people do now. One day the wisest of the creatures, the owl, called a meeting. All the animals and birds gathered in the village center to find out the reason for the convocation.

First the owl warned them that men were moving into their part of the world. He went on to say that these men were hunting the animals and killing them to use as food or to take their skins for clothing. He also explained that this was not bad, since men needed something to eat and clothes to wear, so it was just part of nature's way. There were some men, however who were not showing proper respect for the animals they killed and were wasting the meat and skins. Something had to be done about those men.

That was when the sly fox stepped forward and suggested that each animal and bird pick a disease to carry in its spirit. Then, if a man killed an animal wastefully or without respect, the man would catch the disease carried in that animal's spirit.

All the animals thought that was a good idea and

lined up to pick their disease. The biggest and strongest animals went first, followed by the smaller animals and birds. First the black bear picked, then the panther, the wolf, the bald eagle, and the white-tailed deer. This went on until the little red chipmunk was the last animal in line. When they asked him which disease he wanted, he replied that he did not want one. He then explained that men did not hunt chipmunks for food and his skin was too small to be of use to them. For those reasons he did not need a disease, nor did he want one.

At that the other animals became angry, demanding that the chipmunk take a disease just like the rest of them. Again he refused. The animals then began trying to stomp, bite, and scratch the chipmunk, who was running around in the circle of animals trying to escape. Just as it was about to get away, the panther swiped at the little creature with its claw, leaving scratches down the chipmunk's back. Those scratches then became stripes and have been on chipmunks ever since.

"The Indians had some goofy stories," Brent observed.

"Did you make that up, Dad?" Zane demanded.

"Hey, do I look like an Indian?" was my defense.

"You know anymore of those stories?" Brent asked.

"I thought you said they were goofy?"

"They are, but they're still pretty good," he defended.

"Since we've got such warm sunshine today, I

guess I should tell you how the Cherokees thought the sun got into the sky," I offered. "It also explains why the possum doesn't have hair on his tail."

"This ought to be good," Brent mocked.

Back when the world was first formed, the animals discovered that the sun was stuck on the other side of the world. For that reason it was always daytime over there and nighttime here. As was their custom, all the animals and birds got together and talked about what to do about the problem.

It was finally decided that the bear, being the strongest animal, would be sent around to bring the sun to this side of the world. Off he went, only to return and report that he could not hold the sun since it burned his paws.

Next the eagle was sent to get the sun. He too failed because the sun was too hot to hold in his talons.

Finally the possum stepped forward, threw his long bushy tail proudly into the air and said he would go get the sun. A lot of the animals just snickered since they all knew the possum only was good for sitting around preening the hair on his tail and telling everyone how beautiful it was. But, since they were desperate, they sent the possum.

Soon he returned with the sun! The possum had curled his tail around it and pulled the sun around the world. Unfortunately, the heat of the sun had burned all the hair off his beautiful tail and since that time none has ever grown on a possum's tail.

"That's even lamer than the last one," Brent complained.

"But I know one that you'll probably think is even worse," I warned.

"OK, let's hear it then," he said, feinting a bored indifference.

The Cherokees believed that the feather from a blue jay could have some very magical properties. Since it was the first bird that they saw looking for food each morning or working on its nest, they thought it was the hardest working of all birds.

Whenever they had a child who was lazy and would not get out of bed in the morning, they would make a blue jay potion to cure the laziness. First they would find a blue jay feather. It had to be one that had fallen from a live bird and could not be taken from a dead one. The feather was then ground up and mixed with water to make a paste or potion.

The mother or father of the child would then rub this potion on the child's eyes while it was asleep. The next morning the child would jump out of bed and want to get right to work on its chores. That child would never again be lazy and want to lay in bed.

"Goofiest of all," Brent lamented.

"Is that for real?" Zane asked.

"Sure is," I replied. "I even tried it on you two."

"You did?" Zane asked skeptically.

"Did it work?" Brent chimed in.

"Well, sort of," I smiled. "The next morning after I rubbed it in your eyes, I was awakened early by sounds coming from the backyard. When I got out there both of you were sitting in a tree, squawking and chewing on earthworms."

"Aw, Dad!"

Family Lore

The Marvelous Hoop Snake

Some of my earliest recollections of childhood center on open fireplaces piled high with blazing logs. My family's periodic wintertime, weekend visits with aunts and uncles invariably ended in an evening of staring dreamily into such fires. My 10-year-old imagination searched among the glowing embers for images to match the stories the grown-ups swapped in the dim light.

My father and one of our uncles often sat in overstuffed chairs on either side of the fire, while my brother and I lounged on throw rugs covering pine floorboards. The winter winds rustled the bare tree limbs outside the window, mingling its whistling rush

57

with the clatter of supper dishes being cleared from the table by our mom and aunt in the adjoining dining room.

The heat from the hearth broiled our faces, while our backsides remained slightly chilled. Between the two extremes we were filled with a warm glow, brought on as much by fatigue and a big meal as by the fire. We often were dressed in flannel and denim from a day of hiking in the woods, having shed only our shoes to allow toes to wiggle as the flames warmed our socks.

The room was filled with the tart smell of a golden delicious apple that one of the adults was peeling with slow deliberate strokes of a pocket knife. Quite often that adult was my Uncle Clyde and on those nights there was no shortage of entertainment to be found in the conversation.

My thoughts were recalled from their wanderings among the glowing orange embers by the sounds of an innocent enough question aimed at our uncle.

"Uncle Clyde," my brother asked, "Weren't you afraid that there was a snake down in that hole you dropped your knife in today? You didn't even look in before you reached after it."

"Well, I didn't exactly think about that at the time and I've had this old blade for 30 years. It was given to me by your grandpa and I wasn't about to leave it down in that hole," Uncle Clyde began. "And besides, there wouldn't be a snake in an open hole like that when the weather is as cold as it was today. He'd be buried up in a covered den at this time of year."

While my brother considered the explanation, I leaped into the conversation, moving it deeper into the subject.

"What's the biggest snake you ever saw, Uncle Clyde?" I asked.

My uncle paused from coring the apple and rubbed his grizzled chin as he stared for several moments at some invisible registry of personal history in front of him, through which he mentally rifled for the correct answer.

"I reckon that would have been back when I was a boy just about your age. Your grandpa and I were taking a wagon load of cotton through Brush Bottom over to the gin at Dry Trestle. We were coming through that bottom on the way home about sundown when we saw this snake up ahead. The mules pulling the wagon froze up at the sight of the snake and wouldn't budge another step in that direction.

"Now I can't say exactly how long that critter was since its head was in the bushes on one side of the road and its tail was in the grass on the other side, but I'd guess that the road must have been a good seven or eight feet wide."

"What kind was it?" I asked, as my brother and I leaned in Uncle Clyde's direction.

Knitting his brow and munching a slice of the apple, the man hesitated another long moment as, in turn, he peered into the eyes of each of our young faces. Finally, having apparently seen what he was looking for, he resumed speaking.

"Well, there were several kinds that got mighty big back in those days," he began, "but this one was as black as midnight under a skillet, so I imagine he was a coach whip."

"What did you do?" implored my brother, fidgeting from side to side at the thought of such a monstrous reptile.

"Did you get down and kill him?" I asked.

"No sir!" retorted Uncle Clyde. "It wasn't bothering us, so we just let him take his time and crawl on out of our way. Anyway, you couldn't have paid me to get down on the ground with a coach whip. They're just as likely to chase a man as to look at him.

"Why, I heard of a fellow who met one in a pasture one time and the snake refused to let him pass, so he finally had to just turn around and go back the way he had come. Of course, as soon as he turned his back on the snake, that coach whip lit out after him and chased him across the field. The only way he could get the snake to stop chasing him was to turn and chase it a while. They stayed out there taking turns running each other back and forth across that pasture until it got dark. Then the old snake slipped away, but the man was so tired he just dropped from exhaustion and they found him out there the next morning sound asleep, laying in the grass."

We boys glanced at each other in silence, unsure whether to be amazed or skeptical. We were quickly saved from the situation by our father.

"Humph!" Dad snorted in amusement.

"What's that, Buck?" asked Uncle Clyde.

"I'd wager that whatever was chasing that fellow probably didn't come out of a hole in the ground," Dad said with a trace of a grin. "Sounds more like it came out of a whiskey bottle and was an excuse for not coming home the night before."

"Ahhh, it's a fact," protested Uncle Clyde. "I knew some of the boys that found him."

"Is a coach whip poison, Dad?" I asked over my bother's half-suppressed giggles.

"No, son, the only poison snakes around here are cottonmouths, copperheads, and an occasional timber rattler."

"And the hoop snake," interjected Uncle Clyde matter-of-factly.

"What's a hoop snake?" I asked.

"Never heard of that one!" added my brother.

"Doesn't surprise me that you haven't," answered Uncle Clyde. "You only find them in the piney woods of west Georgia and east Alabama and they've never been very common. And as ornery as they are, it's a good thing that there aren't many of them left."

Dad smiled and shook his head slowly as he settled a little deeper into his easy chair.

"Now, Clyde, you're not going to fill these boy's heads full of any trash, are you?" he chided.

"Nary a word, but the truth," returned Uncle Clyde, trying his best to look offended.

"Clyde, you wouldn't know the truth if it slapped you up side of the head!" Dad shot back with a laugh.

After a moment of silence, I could stand it no longer.

"Tell us about the hoop snake, Uncle Clyde."

"Yes, Clyde, why don't you tell us about this hoop snake," baited Dad.

Uncle Clyde paid no attention to his brother's skeptical tone as he munched another slice of apple before launching forth with his explanation.

"Well, boys, the hoop snake's not like most reptiles. Usually, if you leave them alone, they just naturally don't bother you either, but the hoop snake is so mean that he seems to take pleasure in bedeviling folks whenever he gets the chance. I once heard a preacher say that although it wasn't scriptural, he suspected that Eve's serpent in the Garden of Eden must have been a hoop snake."

"Did you ever know anybody who was bitten by one," asked my brother.

"Oh, the hoop snake doesn't bite. He has a poison spike right on the top of his head that he'll sting you with. See, when he gets mad or just full of mischief, he'll raise up, take his tail in his mouth and go rolling off across country like a barrel hoop. Of course, that's how he came by his name. When he's ready to strike, he'll get a rolling start and spring at you head first."

Uncle Clyde paused for another slice of apple, surveying his audience with a studied and somber expression before continuing.

"He's a black snake and probably related to a coach whip in some way, since he enjoys chasing folks, too. Your grandma had a brother who got chased by one once."

"Did it get him?" I asked.

"Nope. He managed to climb up a tree to get away from it. In fact, I've never known anybody who was actually hit by one, but old man Jim Harris came about as close as you can."

Uncle Clyde halted his narrative for another slice of apple and fell silent as though he planned to drop the subject right there. The ploy quickly produced its desired effect, getting the expected reward from us boys.

"Tell us about him, Uncle Clyde!"

"Yeah, what happened?"

"Well, it was back when your dad and I were young fellows and the family lived on the Lee Place out by Buzzard Mountain," Uncle Clyde began again. "It was the spring that your dad fell off the porch and got his knee busted and your grandpa was down with a bad back. That left me to do all the plowing, so Pa hired old man Jim to come over and help out. One day he was plowing one of the mules on a patch of bottom land between the Seaboard railroad tracks and Clear Creek, where there was a big old black gum tree that stood in the middle of the field by itself. At one end was a bluff that overlooked the bottom. You remember that field, don't you brother?"

Dad shook his head in the affirmative.

"I remember the field, Clyde," he answered, "but that's all I'll vouch for in your tale."

Uncle Clyde plunged ahead with the story, not the least bit deterred by his brother's lack of support.

"Well, about noon old man Jim decided to eat his lunch in the shade of that black gum. He had just got settled down when he looked up on the bluff and saw this hoop snake raise up. It formed a hoop and down the hill it came, straight at him. Now old man Jim was pretty near 70 then, but was still mighty spry and he just managed to get out of the snake's path as it let go of its tail to strike. That snake went right past him like an arrow and drove its spike into that tree. Old man Jim started looking for a strong stick to kill the snake while it was dangling there, but before he could, it worked its way loose and went rolling off across that plowed ground faster than a horse could run."

"Would it have killed him if it had hit him, Uncle Clyde?" I blurted.

"Well, that's hard to say," replied Uncle Clyde. "I don't know if you boys have ever been around any black gums, but those are the hardest trees in the world to kill. In fact, this one had been struck by lightning two or three times without losing a leaf.

"Anyway, old man Jim said that by the time he had scared that snake off and finished eating his lunch that the leaves had already begun to fall off the tree and by the next day it was dead as a doornail. And I know for a fact that after the tree fell over, nothing would ever grow on that spot again."

With that, Uncle Clyde leaned back in his chair and finished off his apple with the confident air of having cleared up all questions concerning the history of the hoop snake.

"You know, Clyde," Dad began, "I believe old man Jim was the one who told his wife he was carried off by a will-o'-the-wisp and held prisoner all night one Halloween."

"Well, yeah, that was him," admitted Uncle Clyde. "He did have a tendency to stretch things a mite from time to time."

"Uh huh," Dad mused. "I never knew of him stretching the truth except when he could get someone to listen to him."

"Ahhh, Buck!" scowled Uncle Clyde good-naturedly as a ripple of laughter emerged from us boys.

Outside the wind continued to rustle the tree branches, while inside the flames still crackled warmly in the fireplace. The talk passed on to other subjects and other times, and for a while I tried to listen. Finally my eyelids grew heavy beyond control. I could hear talk no more as I nodded off into a sound sleep in search of hoop snakes and other wonders.

Possum Tradition

Probably the most common sight along Southern roads and highways these days is the ever-present and thoroughly squashed road-killed possum. You'll notice that I said possum and not "opossum," the way it shows up in a dictionary. As nearly as can be scientifically verified, whatever an opossum is, one has never ventured south of the Mason-Dixon Line.

Let it also be noted, for those who have never encountered the critter in a live condition, that they are not born with tread marks on their backs. These are applied at a later date, usually after dark and near the middle of a roadway.

Although now considered little more than a curiosity, back when I was a boy these marsupials were considered prime game for serious hunters. Up until the 1960s, the hunting of possums was considered just as proper as setting a pack of beagles on the trail of a rabbit.

Now that white-tailed deer have become common throughout the nation, hunters are too busy chasing deer to enjoy a possum hunt. Though you'll still find Br'er Possum in the hunting regulations, it's hard to find anyone who really cares.

Ah, but what of the golden era of possum hunting? From the Great Depression on through World War II and into the 1950s, no self-respecting family farm would be without a possum dog. That situation in large part stemmed from the fact that any four-footed member of the canine family that would chase a possum was the correct breed for the job. Whether they were blue tick, beagle, or mixed mutt, ancestry was never an important part of possum chasing. It seemed as though every farmhouse had a possum dog hiding under the front porch.

Other than rounding up a dog, the only equipment possum hunting required was a kerosene lantern and a croaker sack (which translates into English as a burlap bag). Once dark had descended on the land, it was time to light the lantern, chase the dog from under the porch and head into the woods.

My own earliest recollection of possum hunting finds my father, my brother, a couple of assorted cousins, and myself scouring the west Georgia town of

Rockmart on a 1958 Saturday afternoon in search of a possum dog and its owner to accompany us for the evening's hunt.

A fellow, who I remember only as "Old Luther" and his less than energetic hound were finally located and nightfall found us deep in the woods. After an appropriate amount of aimless wandering in the fields and forests, a random site was chosen to build a camp-fire. Soon yams were roasting in the coals, while an ample supply of apples and peanuts were passed around to satisfy those after-dinner munchies brought on by the walking. While the hunting party was thus engaged, the dog was sent out to bound through the night in search of a possum.

As the noise of our initial wave of gnawing apples and crunching peanuts died away, the conversation opened.

"Tell us a story, Uncle Buck," one of my cousins would begin.

"Yeah, Dad, about when you were a boy and went hunting."

After a measured amount of our pleading, my father would give in and start to reminisce.

"You boys sure had it easy tonight," he offered. "It's not always so simple to get into the woods for the hunt."

"What do you mean?" we ganged up on him.

"I remember once when I was a little older than you boys, your grandpa, my brothers, and I started out on a possum hunt. That was back during the hard times of the Depression and we only got one pair of new overalls each year. I'd just gotten mine and they'd been washed for the first time. That made them shrink just enough to be tight on me.

"Anyway, getting ready to leave, I stuffed my pockets full of apples for when we built the fire. It was early fall, but the night wind was blowing some and the evening was pretty crisp. That cold wind had me cramming my hands in my pockets as well, which made those overalls strain from the load.

"About this time, as we were walking down a two-rut wagon road, I tripped on a root and fell head first into one of those ruts. Laying face down, those overalls were so tight I couldn't get my hands out of the pockets, and because of the way I'd landed, I couldn't roll over either."

"What'd you do, Dad?" I asked.

"I just had to flop around like a catfish out of water until I could work a hand loose. Those worthless brothers of mine were too busy rolling on the ground and laughing to help me up."

"Why, that ain't nothing," Old Luther piped up from his perch on a log across the fire from my father. He then lit into a string of stories about hunts he had been on over the years. Each of them seemed to involve white lightning whiskey, fancy women, or cussing fits, the latter of which Old Luther repeated in great detail. With each tale he told, truth became less and less a part of the their fabric.

It was also obvious that my father was rather

nervous about the subjects being covered in these stories. He was, no doubt, worried that my mother or one of my aunts might get a play-by-play description from one of us boys later on, for which he would end up paying a price.

Occasionally Old Luther would take a break from his stories to let out a "Hunt'em on!" shout at the top of his lungs to encourage the dog in its pursuit. My father took advantage of one of these breaks to reclaim the conversation.

"Don't reckon your dog will be treeing anything tonight," my father observed.

"Why would you say that?" Old Luther asked guardedly.

"Well, he's been laying behind you by a stump, just out of the fire light, for the last hour."

While Old Luther launched into a cussing fit of his own, directed at the dog, he proceeded to chase the unlucky hound out into the night.

"What's treeing mean?" asked one of my cousins, while the dog handler was gone.

"That's when the possum runs up a tree to escape from the dog," my father explained, "although they will sometimes also run down into a hole. You still refer to it as treed, even when that happens. Of course, if that happens tonight, I don't think we'll help Luther dig the critter out. I'm not sure that mutt of his would know the difference between a possum and a skunk."

After our laughter had died down, and Old Luther had returned to again launch into a tall tale, we were interrupted by the dog howling out in the woods.

"He's treed," Old Luther cried. "Let's go get him."

"Dad, how are we going to kill the possum? We didn't even bring a gun," I asked, as we trooped through the woods behind the dog handler and his lantern.

My father explained that guns were not needed since we were going to take the possum alive. Since these creatures are the garbage disposals of the forest, they will eat any type of carrion or other disgusting bits of food they find. While their diet poses no health threat to anyone planning to eat one, many possum hunters claim the meat ordinarily has a wild and unpleasant taste. For that reason the critter is taken alive, kept in a pen for a week or so and fed table scraps to fatten it and improve the taste.

By this time we had located the dog at the foot of a tree in a creek bottom. The tree was heavily covered with several types of clinging vines. The lantern's glow reflected off the eyes of a possum perched on a limb half way up the tree.

"How are we going to get him down?" I asked.

"I'll go up and shake him off his limb," Old Luther replied. "When he hits the ground he'll just roll over and 'play possum.' Then y'all can pick him up by the tail and put him in the croaker sack."

It all sounded reasonable enough as we crowded around the trunk of the tree to watch Old Luther's ascent. It quickly developed that among the clinging vines was at least one variety with thorns. We were treated to another dose of Old Luther's polished cussing as he climbed. When the proper limb was reached, the possum was shook off of it and the dog handler slide back down the trunk through the vines, again cussing all the way.

Meanwhile, the possum had fallen into a tangle of honeysuckles and briars beneath the tree. The dog, my father, and all of us boys dove in after it to see who would capture the beast. When the proverbial dust had settled, the lantern light revealed some very scratched and perplexed hunters and the dog, but the possum was no where to be found. It had quietly escaped beneath the vine tangle during the commotion, proving that not all possums know they are supposed to play dead when cornered.

Looking back, it now occurs to me that the possum hunts I have been on or have heard recounted very rarely ended with the possum actually going home with the hunters. That could be because, after the joy of such hunts, most outdoorsmen could not face the added fun of skinning and cooking a possum. But those chores are a story in themselves and best left for another time.

Turtle Grabbing

The rhythmic jerking finally yanked Buck from the depths of a deep sleep and he opened his eyes to see his Uncle Paul standing at the foot of the bed. Uncle Paul was already dressed in ill-fitted overalls and a slouch hat. The man had both the occupants of the feather mattress by their respective big toes and was shaking the boys to wake them.

"Come on, Buck. You and Clyde roll out of there. It's getting late."

Through the open window Buck could see the big slice of moon still hanging high in the August night sky as he and his brother began the first squirming of a new day.

"What time is it, Uncle Paul?" Clyde asked sleepily.

"Way past reveille and getting later," the older man hissed back in a whisper. "Y'all get out of there before we waste the whole morning. We got some turtles to catch before noon."

The reminder of the days plan was enough to stir the two boys into meaningful activity. They soon cleared the bed, had shirts and overalls on and their feet were softly padding down the central hall of the house, following their uncle back to the kitchen.

As the boys headed out the rear door toward the small wooden building at the back of the yard, Uncle Paul halted them for a second.

"Give me your handkerchiefs and I'll pack us some lunch," he commanded.

The handkerchiefs were surrendered from hip pockets and the two brothers continued their errand. When they reentered the kitchen, the glow of a kerosene lantern spread its flickering light throughout the room. On the table in the middle of the room three places were set with plates containing big saucer-sized homemade biscuits stuffed with fried slabs of fat back bacon. Next to them were glasses of fresh milk. Beside each of the settings lay the handkerchiefs, wrapped around a couple more portions of the biscuits and meat.

The boys slid into their chairs on opposite sides of their already seated uncle.

"Lord, make us grateful for what we have, amen," Uncle Paul pronounced while they all bowed their heads. "Now get at it, boys. Time's wasting."

Between mouthfuls Buck directed a question at the older man.

"How long before you have to get back to the army, Uncle Paul?"

"I report back to McPherson down in Atlanta in 10 days," he replied in his usual clipped manner of speaking. "I'll take the train down a week from Wednesday."

"Are you always going to be a soldier, Uncle?" Clyde asked.

"Probably so. It's the only thing I've ever done since joining up for the big war. It's been a way to see a lot of the world. As hard as times are now, a man can't find any other work anyway, so I reckon I'll hang on for my pension."

"Ma says you stay in because you're to high and mighty to be a farmer," Buck said.

"Your ma's like most folks. She don't think much of soldiering when there's not a war to be fought. But everybody's not cut out for making a crop the way your pa is. Being brothers-in-law don't make us much alike," Uncle Paul mused. "Now finish off those biscuits and let's hit the road before everybody's out of bed and they try to put us to work."

The trio was soon headed across the front yard, their lunches in the breast pockets of their overalls. Clyde carried a burlap croaker sack, while an old hound tagged along in the party's wake.

"Run that old dog back to the house," Uncle Paul commanded. "That animal's about the most useless dog the Lord ever allowed on Earth."

"Won't do no good," Clyde pointed out. "She'd just stay a little further back and follow us anyway."

The ridge line to the east was now beginning to glow from the great orange globe of the sun that still hid just beyond the crest. Little swirls of dust kicked up each time the boy's bare feet struck the dirt road they now followed, as it cut a swath through the alternating corn and cotton fields.

"Will you come back here to live when the army let's you go, Unc?" Buck asked after a mile or so of silent pacing down the road.

"Never really thought about it," his uncle replied. "Don't know where else I'd go. All the family's here and I still know most of the folks in the county. I've seen some mighty pretty towns and some big fancy cities, but they were just places to visit. I wasn't part of them."

"Shoot, we can't wait until pa says we're old enough to take off for Atlanta," Clyde said.

"I wouldn't be in too big a rush to grow up if I were you fellows," Paul pointed out.

"You were only five years older than us when you went to the war," Buck argued.

"That's true, but I had to lie about my age since they wouldn't take anybody until they turned 18. That was before I knew the value of being truthful," Paul countered. "Besides, there's not a war going on and even if there was, we've got more sense now than to get into another fight between kings and kaisers."

"We're still going to Atlanta," Clyde stated.

"That's between you and your pa," Uncle Paul concluded. "All I'm doing is taking you turtling."

After a couple of more miles of silent walking through the morning mist, the snake-like course of Clear Creek came into view, writhing off to either side of the shallow gravel ford where the road crossed.

Uncle Paul reached into his pocket and tossed his pocket knife to Buck, then plopped down on the road cut and began unlacing his boots.

"You boys find us some good green sticks to poke the turtles, while I get these boots off," he directed.

The boys were soon back with three freshly cut sticks in hand. Uncle Paul took one of these and waded into the creek, his boot laces tied together and the boots draped around his neck. The boys followed a couple of respectable steps behind him, while the hound dog stayed high and dry on the bank but kept pace with their movement upstream. The wading was cool in the morning air, but the sun was now just above the tree line to the east and promised another scorching summer day.

"What do we do next?" Clyde quizzed.

"I can hardly believe that your pa has never taught you fellows how to grab turtles."

"He stays real busy in the fields," Buck answered. "When he does go hunting or fishing it's with the men and he says we're not old enough to go with them yet. Heck, we're just glad he let us off from helping him today so we could come."

"How's he expect you to learn anything that way?"

Uncle Paul scowled. "I expect that I'll have to talk to him about that."

As they waded into the pool at the first curve of the stream, the water came up to over their knees. Uncle Paul bent over and poked his stick up under the over hanging bank on the outside bend of the shore. The old slouch hat he had borrowed from his brother-in-law hid his face from the boys.

"You see fellows," their uncle began, "when you hit something hard with the end of the stick, you know that it is either a rock or a turtle."

Uncle Paul suddenly retracted the stick, switched it to his left hand and jammed his now free right one up under the bank. When his hand broke the water's surface on its way back from under the bank, a soft-shelled turtle the size of a small frying pan was held firmly in his grasp.

"There's the first one. Open our croaker sack, Clyde, and I'll drop him in."

The boy responded to the command and watched admiringly as the turtle disappeared into the bag.

"How'd you know which end of the critter you had?" Buck asked.

"Don't really matter with a soft-shell turtle," his uncle advised. "They don't bite much. Now if it had been an old snapper, I'd have felt which way the points on his shell were running. All the points on him point to the back. Usually a turtle will go under the bank head first so you don't need to worry much about whether you are grabbing him by the head."

"What if the points are headed the wrong way?" Clyde intoned.

"Then you let go mighty quick and get your hand out of there. That turtle will be more surprised than you are and you'll have a second or two before he figures out what to do," Uncle Paul continued to explain. "That is, unless you happen to grab him right on the head."

"What happens then?" Buck asked pensively, as though he feared to hear the answer.

"Well, he chomps down on your hand and you have to wait until he hears thunder before he'll turn you loose," the man returned lightly, with a twinkle in his eye. "One of you boys want to try the next one?"

"Not yet," Clyde said.

"Better watch you on a couple more before I try," Buck agreed.

The next hour passed with the creek giving up a couple of more small turtles to the trio, as they waded upstream with the man continuing to do the grabbing. The boys were now beginning to make their first cautious attempts at poking under the banks with the sticks. At this point, though still early in the morning, their uncle called for a rest break and the three of them, along with the hound, sprawled under a big oak tree on the shore.

"Looks like old Daisy is about worn out already," Clyde observed, scratching the old dog's neck. "She must have been out all night chasing a coon or possum."

"Humph," Uncle Paul snorted. "That lazy beast

wouldn't chase a biscuit if you rolled it in front of her. Don't understand why y'all keep that dog around. I got no use for anything that don't pull its weight."

"Old Daisy's a good one," Buck defended. "She's just getting a little old."

"We're going to have to do better ourselves," Uncle Paul observed, changing the subject. "We haven't got nearly enough turtles to make a meal of yet. Of course, that might be because I'm the only one grabbing any."

With that he rose and headed back to the water. At the stream's edge he paused to survey the long stretch of water that spread before them in a still, dark sheet, unbroken as it curled beneath the shade around the next upstream bend of the creek.

"How deep's the water through here?" he asked over his shoulder to the boys.

"Not bad," Buck replied, having no real notion of the actual depth.

No sooner had the answer left the boy's lips than Uncle Paul stepped off the bank into the stream. Without a splash; indeed, almost without a ripple, he slid into the water and disappeared beneath the surface. Only the borrowed slouch hat remained on the water to mark his point of entry.

At first the two youngsters were stunned by the sudden disappearance of their older companion, but when he surfaced gagging, they were overcome by a wave of mirth. Within seconds they were literally rolling on the ground, enveloped in laughter.

"You looked like the fountain in the park over at county seat when you spit out that stream of water, Uncle Paul," Clyde managed through the tears brought on by his laughter.

"Goll darn it, Buck! You knew that hole was over a man's head!" their uncle seethed as he pulled himself out onto a nearby rock that broke the surface of the water. "I ought to take a strap to you, you whimper snapper!"

"My lunch is soaked," he added in a surprised tone as he pulled it from the breast pocket of his overalls.

Seating himself on the rock, the older man began unwrapping the handkerchief.

"What're you doing, Uncle Paul?" Buck finally asked, getting control of himself.

"I'm eating my goll darn lunch before it completely spoils," he snapped back at the boy. "Your daddy obviously hasn't taught you young ones about respecting your elders, has he? You're rolling around over there, carrying on like a couple of hyena dogs."

From that point Uncle Paul stormed off into a long speech about 'this younger generation.' The longer he preached the more agitated he became, still perched on his midstream pulpit rock. Soon his stream of thought had him cussing some of the local county politicians, progressing on up to the state level, and blistering the Depression as well. After grieving over the general state of civilization for a few minutes, he finally concluded with a good tongue lashing of the President of the United States. In the end he laid the blame for all the country's ills and his own recent dunking at the door of the Republican Party in general and President Hoover specifically.

During his monologue, the boys got control of themselves and settled in to go ahead and eat their own lunches, even though it was not yet mid-morning. Sitting in awe, they exchanged admiring glances as they listened to a finer cussing fit than they had ever imagined possible. To them it mirrored all the refinement that only could be gained by a life of travel, as it alluded to places and things with which they were totally unfamiliar.

At the end of his free-flowing speech, Uncle Paul surveyed the surrounding water and finally found a route to the shore that kept his head above the surface. On the bank he put his now wet boots back on and immediately turned downstream toward the road.

"Where you headed?" Buck yelled after him.

"To the house," was his only reply.

"What should we do with the turtles?" Clyde called, looking into the sack.

This set Uncle Paul off on another disjointed dialogue, this time on the shortcomings of the animal kingdom. Included in his thoughts was the suggestion that the miserable creatures in the bag be tossed back into the creek.

"Just as well," Clyde noted. "Daisy's so tuckered out that we'll need to carry her in the croaker sack anyway."

When the threesome hit the road, Uncle Paul

refused to let the boys walk with him, relegating them to following him at a distance. Thus they proceeded, Uncle Paul in the lead, still soaked, with the slouch hat drooping on his head. The boys loped along behind him, taking turns carrying the sack over their shoulder, from which Daisy's head and front paws protruded.

If the youngsters ventured too close, it would provoke musings from Uncle Paul about the insanity that must run through the family in light of his being out on the road with a couple of half wits who had a dog in a sack. Of course, Buck and Clyde would close the gap ever so often just to be entertained.

The morning calm was broken as they neared the spot where the Seaboard Railroad crossed the dusty road. From behind them came the sputtering sound of a T-Model Ford approaching. As it chugged past the boys the lone occupant eyed the pair, but kept moving. The vehicle overtook Uncle Paul at the rail crossing.

"Is that you, Paul?" the driver called. "What happened to you? You're soaked. Come on in here and I'll give you a ride."

Uncle Paul climbed aboard nodding his appreciation, but offering no explanation.

"Where you going this morning?" the driver continued to question.

"Up to my sister's place will be fine, Mr. Greer," Uncle Paul stated.

"Isn't that your sister's two boys back there in the road?" the driver asked. "It looked sort of like they had a hound dog in that burlap bag?"

"I haven't ever seen those two gypsies before," Uncle Paul replied curtly.

As the boys watched the dust cloud of the automobile moving away, Clyde spoke first.

"You think Uncle Paul had a good time?"

"I don't know," Buck replied. "Hard to tell about old folks sometimes."

The Battle of Pegimore Creek

Most Southern boys growing up in the 1950s and 60s spent many summer afternoons playing 'army.' One reason for this game of imitating soldiers probably came from the stories of military life we were told by our elders. Whether the tales were about the Civil War and General Stonewall Jackson, or about our own fathers and uncles in World War II at places like Midway or Bastogne, we all heard the stories and refought the battles in our backyards.

My brother and I were blessed with one family story that set us apart, however, from our friends in the neighborhood. Our family had a direct link to the Battle of Pegimore Creek.

Before you spend too much time looking up this fight in history books, don't bother. You won't find it there, since it was not a battle between great armies. It was actually a small clash between man and nature, and one from which mankind retreated a bit more humble. Like most great battles, this one started quite by accident.

"Uncle Paul, it's too hot to be climbing through these briar patches," Buck complained, as he struggled to pull himself free from the clutches of a dried blackberry cane. "Can't we head back down to Clear Creek and go swimming?"

"It is a bit unseasonable for this time of year," the older man conceded as he wiped the late September sweat from his brow with a red handkerchief. "Still, we've got to bring something home for your ma to cook for supper."

"Ouch! If I'd known we were going traipsing through the briars, I'd have stayed home or got ma to let me wear my shoes," Clyde added to the complaint. "I don't think there's even a groundhog in the county anyway. We sure haven't seen any."

"Just now getting to the best hunting ground," Uncle Paul answered. "There's pasture land up ahead on the Johnson place and the groundhogs have their borrows in the banks along the creek valley up there. But, we won't find any standing here jawing."

The man picked up the battered 10-gauge, double-barreled shotgun he had leaned against a stump during the break. Turning upstream he led the way along the edge of tiny Pegimore Creek.

"Sure wish this creek was big enough for swimming," Buck lamented as he fell in line.

"Or at least wading," Clyde grumbled.

"You two are worse than a couple of old church ladies," Uncle Paul growled as he forged ahead.

After a few more minutes of walking and sweating, a high bank presented itself on the group's right, just downstream of the point where the creek flowed out of the Johnson pasture and into the woods. Several obvious groundhog holes were visible in the bank, as well as a couple of small rocky crevices. Uncle Paul leaned his shotgun across a rock and climbed the steep face to look for signs of recent groundhog activity around the holes.

As he approached one of the rocky openings, he suddenly cocked his head to the side, striking a listening pose.

"You boys break me off a muskrat brush and bring it up here," he commanded over his shoulder. "I think I hear one hiding in this rock hole."

Buck dutifully pulled out his pocket knife and cut a limb off a nearby hawthorn bush. The limb was covered with the two-inch spikes that give the plant its nickname, since they would be ideal for combing the hair on the back of that aquatic rodent.

"What are you going to do, Unc?" Buck asked as he carried the limb up to the man, followed closely but tentatively by his brother.

"I'm going to twist the rascal out of there," he replied, taking the stick from his nephew and jamming it into the hole.

Immediately a shriek came from the opening. The sound was an unearthly wail, sounding much like fingernails being raked across a blackboard. Uncle Paul and his companions leaped back away from the hole, expecting some underworld demon to pounce out upon them.

"Hot dang!" Uncle Paul shouted. "I believe there's a tiger in there."

Having never seen or heard a tiger, the boys went along with there uncles opinion. After all, he had seen much of the world, and even been to Europe once.

"Let's get out of here," Clyde pleaded.

"Or at least go get the shotgun," Buck added.

"Wait a minute," Uncle Paul countered, approaching the hole again and bending over it, while still clutching the hawthorn limb. "That looks like - it is a nest full of baby buzzards in there! Never knew those things could make such a racket."

The boys now got up their nerve and crept forward to peer at the nest.

"They sure are cute little fellows," Clyde observed. "Wonder if they'd make good pets?"

"Would if you like to chew road kill," Uncle Paul stated.

"What do you mean?" Buck asked.

"A momma buzzard finds dead meat, eats it, then flies back to the nest to throw it up to feed the little ones."

"You mean they eat vomit?" both boys blurted out together.

"That's about the size of it," their uncle smiled. "Only it smells worse. Remember, the meat was already rotting when the buzzard found it and then it goes through the birds innards."

Just then a black shadow floated across the ground straight at the trio. Instinctively they all looked up to see a couple of adult buzzards beginning to circle low over them. Higher up several more of the ominous scavengers glided on the air currents, drawing nearer.

"Must be about feeding time," Uncle Paul said. "We better be moving on."

He had hardly finished the sentence when the nearest of the buzzards broke into a steep dive directly at the man and boys.

"God Almighty, it's coming for us!" Uncle Paul shouted just before the buzzard's feet knocked his hat off. At the same time the black, outstretched wings smacked against the faces of the boys on either side.

Uncle Paul let out a blasphemous curse as the second buzzard dove to the attack. The man raised the muskrat brush he still held and began to flail violently in the air, trying to ward off the attacker. Quickly the other buzzards began dropping into the melee, as the two boys thrashed their arms about their heads to beat off the foul-breathed harpies.

The action was going nicely, with the man and boys retreating slowly down the bank, holding their own against the airborne attack. In fact, the first two birds broke off and landed at the hole to check the nest, while the other buzzards continued to harass the intruders. At this point, however, matters took a turn for the worse.

One particularly bedraggled bird who was the largest in the flock came straight for Uncle Paul. As it prepared to pull out of its dive, Uncle Paul swung at it with his muskrat brush and connected. The buzzard was immediately tangled in the large thorns and tumbled headlong into Uncle Paul's chest, sending both man and bird to the ground.

As mentioned earlier, regurgitation is the chosen method that buzzards employ in feeding their young, but it is also their most effective means of defense at close quarters. Many unfortunate persons who have had close encounters with buzzards have come away awed by the accuracy with which the birds can hit a target up to 10 or 12 feet distant. Uncle Paul, finding himself entangled at extremely close quarters, had no chance at all. Instantly he was covered with the most foul concoction imaginable, as the buzzard unloaded on him.

Since the rest of the flock had retreated when the man and bird became entangled, the boys were free to enjoy the show and break into loud and long laughter at the sight. Naturally, this infuriated their uncle even more at his predicament, prompting an outbreak of cussing that would befit a man who had spent years traveling the world collecting foul language as a member of Uncle Sam's army.

When the man and buzzard were finally freed of

each other the bird tried to escape by taking flight. Uncle Paul, meanwhile, found himself at the bottom of the bank and lying beside the shotgun. Immediately leaping to his feet, Uncle Paul brought the scatter gun to his shoulder and let fly with both barrels at the fleeing bird. The kick of the double-barrel blast knocked Uncle Paul backward, sending him sprawling into the clutches of a tangle of blackberry briars. As he landed he let out a shriek that dwarfed that of the baby buzzards.

"You missed, Unc...," Buck began to say, but he did not finish the sentence.

As the load of buckshot zipped past the buzzard, the bird's queasy stomach again responded.

"Yuck," both boys groaned as they joined their uncle in being drenched with the contents of the fleeing buzzard's stomach.

Buck and Clyde's mother stared bewildered at the sight approaching her across the yard. Uncle Paul led the way, dressed in his boots and red flannel, long underwear, dripping wet and carrying the shotgun. Close behind followed the two wet boys, in their underwear and looking quite sheepish.

"Don't even ask," Uncle Paul snorted at his sister as he entered the house. "Our clothes are soaking down in the creek."

As the boys came onto the porch their mother eyed them reproachfully.

"I don't know what happened, but I think you two

are spending entirely too much time around that worthless brother of mine," she scolded as the boys attempted to keep straight faces in order to avoid getting their mother any more riled up.

Peach State Rabbit Tales

Growing up in suburban Atlanta in the 1950s created a bit of a culture clash. Though living in an in-town household, our family was still but one generation away from the farm and rural life. In fact, such situations were not at all uncommon in that day. The unpleasantness of the 1940s known as World War II had been the catalyst for sending thousands of Southerners scurrying from the farm into towns and cities to work in armament plants and, after the war, industrial jobs.

These folks, of course, did not leave behind all of their cultural attachments. One that was commonly brought along was the love of the outdoors in general and of hunting in particular. Such was the case in our family during my formative years. Prior to moving to

Atlanta my father had grown up on a west Georgia farm during the Great Depression. He had learned to hunt to help feed the family, as well as for recreation. His love of the outdoors naturally passed along to his offspring.

In that period, neither deer nor turkeys had been restocked in Georgia, so they were not even considered when a hunt was being planned. In an urban or suburban setting it was pretty impractical to keep a bird dog, so quail were game birds of chance that were stumbled onto by accident during hunts.

As a result, this was the heyday of rabbit hunting. Naturally, the most effective method of hunting was using a pack of beagles to find and run the critters. Again, however, these diminutive, yelping hounds were not ideal neighbors, so, in the interest of peace in the neighborhood, hunting dogs were rarely available to us.

Fortunately, most rural areas where row cropping was common in that decade were overrun with cottontails. It was relatively easy to put on a "rabbit drive" and be quite successful. And, back then, farmers were more than happy to allow hunters to thin out the bunnies on their land. One only needed to politely ask permission and remember to close the gates to stay on good terms with most landowners.

Our family rabbit hunts usually were composed of my father, brother, myself and an assorted gaggle of uncles and cousins. We would spread out to walk in line, stretched over a swath of 75 or 100 feet along the edges of fields and pastures. Undoubtedly, many cottontails simply stayed hidden and let us walk past them, but back then the rabbits were so thick that enough were jumped to keep the action at an adequate, if not constant level.

My first rabbit was taken on such a hunt when I was about 12 years old. He was one of those cottontails that preferred stealth, but I caught sight of him slipping into a ditch full of blackberry canes. The single-shot .410 shotgun I carried changed the critter's plans and the rabbit went home to dinner with a proud and excited young hunter.

Another bonus of springing from a rabbit hunting family was the wealth of tales that were bandied about the fireplace on winter evenings. Listening to the stories of hunts from bygone days was about as much fun for preteen boys as were the actual days in the field.

One that was retold more than once around the hearth dealt with a hunt my father, Rufus Jacobs, was on that demonstrated just how plentiful cottontails once were in the Peach State. He and a group of his cronies were putting on a drive up a west Georgia hollow that bordered some farmland. Suddenly, from the bottom of the mini ravine, a cottontail bolted in front of my dad. Throwing his 12-gauge to his shoulder, he sang out "there he goes!" He also let loose a load of No. 6 shot at the fleeing rabbit.

"You got him!" shouted one of his hunting buddies.

Needless to say that proved rather confusing to my father, since he was watching the rabbit disappear farther down the hollow on the run.

"Nope, I missed him," Dad corrected.

"I see him and he's dead as a door nail," the crony argued.

Sure enough, there was a dead rabbit on the side of the hollow, but it was one that had been sitting in its bed. My dad's shot at the running rabbit had sailed high to strike the cottontail trying to hide in the cover!

Back in those days, my father was a rather large man (affectionately referred to as "Lard" by his brothers and friends), and not above adding a bit of humor to a day in the woods. On one occasion a local Baptist preacher, who was new to the area, mentioned that, although he did not hunt, he enjoyed tagging along on rabbit hunts for the camaraderie and because he did love fried rabbit. He even volunteered to carry all the game in return for an invitation to join a hunt. Obligingly, my dad arranged for the parson to take part in the next outing.

When the appointed day arrived, the weather turned off unseasonably warm for a Piedmont day in the fall. Soon after the hunt began the participants trudged across a dirt road. As my father crossed he spotted a none-to-fresh rabbit laying in the road where it had been run over by a car. Realizing the preacher was not in sight, Dad sang out that he saw a rabbit, discharged a load of shot into the ground and picked up the road kill. The cottontail, complete with tread marks, was handed over to the minister, who dutifully carried it around the rest of the day - until the growing rancid odor of the animal gave the joke away.

Not all of the stories generated in the family by rabbit hunting originate with my father. Probably the most renowned one involved him only in a peripheral way. The hero of this tale was my maternal grandfather, Jim Hannah.

Granddad was a throw back to another age. He was strict, solemn, straight laced and serious, especially when hunting or fishing. Often I accompanied him to some angling destination and less than half a dozen words were exchanged once the water was reached. He thought noise in general and talking in particular scared the fish away. He sat perfectly still and silent for hours waiting for a fish to happen by and bite his hook.

On the memorable hunt, Mr. Hannah (as he was referred to by all of his sons in-law) was in the woods with my dad and a couple of my uncles. They were driving a creek bottom that lies in the shadow of Buzzard Mountain, just outside the town of Rockmart in eastern Polk County. The shooting had been good, with several cottontails already in the game bag.

Suddenly, Granddad let out the familiar call of "There he goes!" Inexplicably, however, there was no report of a shotgun following the yell, which left the other hunters scratching their collective heads. They could see Mr. Hannah locked in a shooting position and looking rather puzzled.

"Where'd he go?" my father finally shouted over to the older man.

"Up that tree!" was the perplexed answer that floated back.

When the hunters gathered under the tree in question they quickly located a fairly ill-tempered old tabby cat looking down at them.

After an appropriate amount of snickering the hunt was resumed, leaving Granddad muttering the rest of the day about how close he came to taking a stray cat home in his game bag!

Now days it is much less common to create a rabbit hunting tradition or to keep it alive in a suburban family. I have tried it with my two sons, but the result has not been very encouraging. We are at the mercy of finding someone who has some beagles for such a hunt. On the occasions when we have tried a rabbit drive the shooting has been intolerable slow and sporadic. There are just too few cottontails in most areas for such tactics to bare fruit.

Of course, when sitting around a campfire, little has changed. I simply dip into the deep well of traditional family rabbit hunting adventures. The next generation of Jacobs boys seem to find them just as entertaining as I did at their age.

Loose Ends

The Cultural History of Grits

It is possible to tell much about a society's culture by looking at what they like to eat. The Japanese are fond of eating raw fish called sushi. The Irish love their corn beef and cabbage, and, of course, we Southerners have our grits. Making light of a people's favorite food is much like making fun of those folks as well. So why is it that non-Southerners heap so much ridicule on grits? Actually, the ridicule is bad enough, but they also insist upon heaping jelly, sugar, catsup and all manner of other ingredients on grits in trying to adapt them to their own tastes. I once knew a native of Korea who doused his morning grits with a dose of soy sauce!

As if these insults were not bad enough, virtually

no one born outside the South has the slightest idea from what plant grits spring, let alone the ability to surmise what is done to make the grain into grits. Don't even think about mentioning hominy in polite conversation with these uninformed Yankees. It would rate right alongside a discussion at the breakfast table of the process involved in making sausage. Hominy, you might say, is the Jurassic ancestor of grits, yet Northerners show a total lack of understanding of this link.

Given this lack of respect and understanding of the grain that gives us such pleasure when smothered with melted butter at breakfast or mixed with cheese and served with biscuits and gravy at dinner, is it surprising that we sometimes become frustrated with our northern neighbors? Rather than trying to explain grits to them, it is so much easier to simply point to the nearest flowering mimosa tree and tell them it is a grit tree in bloom, preparing to bring forth another bountiful crop.

All too often I have heard visitors to the South say that the love of grits is an acquired taste that has never caught on in the northern states. That, of course, is hogwash. Many times I have explained to these folks that the truth of the matter lies in the fact that no one, in spite of many attempts, has ever been able to produce a grit picking machine. This leaves handpicking as the only alternative, which limits the size of each year's grit crop. With such a valuable item that is in short supply, are we likely to ship any north of the Mason-Dixon Line? No sir, I think not! We will contentedly savor them ourselves and let the heathens eat oatmeal.

For the most part, Southerners are very tolerant of Yankees who misunderstand grits. Still, there are limits even to the polite patience we extend to those folks. Several years ago a friend of mine hosted some guests from that benighted land of Lincoln known as Illinois. My friend asked if the visitors would care to have a portion of grits with their first breakfast in the South.

"No," replied one of the Illinoisans. "I've never eaten any and don't believe I'd like them. But, perhaps, I will try just one grit."

One grit! No doubt such scallywags also make fun of motherhood, spit on the flag, and hate baseball. It is enough to make Stonewall Jackson roll over in his grave, if not rise up and chase the barbarian back across the Ohio River.

Just the mention of General Jackson brings to mind a myth concerning the late unpleasantries with our northern neighbors that they are fond of calling the Civil War. For years the story has been told that Southerners claim the Confederate Army under General Robert E. Lee did not actually surrender to General U.S. Grant. The facts are said to show that Grant stole General Lee's sword and, since Lee was much too polite a gentleman to demand it back, the Southern army simply went home, leaving the Yankees to claim a victory in the war. We Southerners have never made such a ridiculous claim.

Like most myths, however, there is a grain of truth in the story. The grain in this case is grits. Let's set the record straight with regard to this misunderstanding.

In the spring of 1865 as the Confederate Army bravely held off the invading Union hordes at Petersburg, Virginia, a stalemate had developed. Often the opposing armies' earthworks were only yards apart, within easy hailing distance. Among the throng of soldiers was a young private, barely 17 years old and freshly mustered into the Federal army. While on guard duty one night he spied a Confederate sentry.

"Hey, Reb," the boy called across no-man's land.

"What can I do for you," came the reply from the Southerner. Unlike the young Union soldier who wore a new blue uniform and carried freshly issued equipment, the rebel soldier was middle aged, with a grizzled face hardened by three years in the field. His uniform was a collection of butternut brown and gray rags and his equipment meager.

"Why are you fellows still fighting?" asked the boy. "You're all but out of food and supplies. Your uniforms are worn out. You can't possibly beat us."

"Well, I reckon we'll keep right on fighting as long as you folks keep coming south. We don't cotton to anybody breaking into our homes and that's the way we've felt about you since you crossed the Potomac River."

After a few moments of silence, the Confederate soldier spoke again.

"What are you fighting for, boy?"

"To save the Union and end slavery," the trooper piped up.

"Well, dagnabit," came the surprised reply from

the veteran rebel. "We thought you boys were trying to steal our grits."

Later that night the news of this conversation was reported back to General Lee's headquarters. After discussing it with his staff, the general announced that the whole war had been an unfortunate misunderstanding and everyone might as well go home. By morning the gray-clad army had broken up into small groups of men headed back to home and family.

At dawn General Grant sent out his usual foraging parties in search of local whiskey stills. Their goal was to return to Union headquarters with enough jugs of white lightning to give General Grant and his officers enough nerve for another day of battle.

Of course, the scouts found the Southerners gone. When the Yankees probed further down the road to Appomattox Courthouse, in their usual rude manner, they kicked in the door and found a rusted sword laying on a table in the building. It was the sword of a Union officer who had recently surrendered to the Southern army, but when Grant saw it he declared it was Robert E. Lee's. Naturally, General Lee chose the gentlemanly path and never publicly disputed the claim. What would have been the point? After all, the grits were now safe.

Whether you accept that version of the story or not, the fact remains that Yankees still misunderstand the Southerner's attachment to grits. My own experience demonstrates this as well.

After a number of years of working for a large company in its Atlanta office, the headquarters of the firm in Chicago decided to move the operation I worked in to that city. A group of personnel folks traveled down to Atlanta to interview all the affected employees. When my turn came I was ushered in and seated across a table from a sour-faced lady in a black business suit. She curtly informed me that I was one of the lucky ones who had a job waiting for me in Chicago. She then began explaining the details of my impending move to the Windy City.

"Excuse me, ma'am," I interrupted.

"Yes, what is it?" she snapped.

"I'd sooner kiss a pig than move to Chicago," I pointed out, watching a look of surprise creep across her face. "I'm not going anywhere I can't buy grits straight off the supermarket shelf."

Needless to say, my interview proved to be a short one. I never got the chance to see the sun rising over Lake Michigan through the window of a commuter train on my way to work. On the other hand, I have been able to get a bowl of grits anytime I wanted one in the ensuing years. Sounds like a fair trade to me.

A Boy And His Pet

Of all the duets that take center stage from time to time, none is more basic than a boy and his dog. Here is friendship at its very best. Inseparable pals, never asking anything save attendance from each other, they float carelessly on the tides of life. Whether the boy is bookish or rough hewn, the dog, mutt or pedigreed, the result is the same. Boy and animal are bonded into a single functioning unit.

To deny a son the chance to claim the title of pet owner would be almost as unthinkable as despising mom, hating baseball, and turning down apple pie. Based on these views of cohabitation with a pet, I looked forward to the day when my youngest son,

Zane, would ask for his first dog. I was completely flexible on the subject, standing equally ready to agree to a Brittany spaniel, retriever, or a beagle. Whether bird dog or hound, I felt sure we would enjoy transforming the pet into a working hunting dog.

Like any loving parent in modern-day America, however, I did harbor the secret fear that Zane might go astray. What if he, God forbid, asked for a Chihuahua or a poodle? Get thee behind me, inconceivable thought! Although various members of the extended family have from time to time provided some pretty convincing evidence that our strain might host a few weak genes, none have ever give indications of really serious brain disorders. For that reason, I rested confident in the knowledge my son would do the family proud, as we Southerners are fond of describing it.

Of course, he would have to be the one to initiate the idea. That way I would have leverage when it came time to discuss feeding, bathing, and cleaning up behind a puppy.

"Remember son, it was your idea to have a dog."

How often I had practiced the line. The greatest of Shakespearean actors never spent more time seeking a more correct delivery. I was ready when the day finally came. Well, at least I thought I was prepared.

Birthday number ten was close at hand and much of Zane's waking time was invested in deciding what he wanted for a present. Then, at long last, the request for a pet was forthcoming.

"Dad, I've decided what I want for my birthday," he stated.

"That's fine, son. What'll it be?" I asked confidently.

"I want a pet."

Oh joyous day, the moment had arrived!

"Can I have a snake or a lizard?"

It must have been something he inherited from the in-laws! Or perhaps it was the result of his Great-Great-Uncle Paul having eaten snakes when he was in the Orient in the army?

"Are you sure, son? Wouldn't a dog be less trouble?"

"I'm sure, Dad, a snake or a lizard."

Thus began my quest for a birthday present pet for the boy. It was quickly pointed out to us by his mother that the new addition to the household would most definitely not be a snake. All members of this family unit were required to possess a minimum of a couple of legs, but no more than four. Both snakes and insects were ruled out.

Beginning the research necessary for finding the right critter soon revealed two drawbacks to most lizards as well. Either the little reptiles tended to bite the hand that fed them, as in the case of geckos and monitors, or they required the forbidden live insects for food (as in the case of true chameleons or anoles). These habits of the mouth eliminated all of those lizards. At last, however, the green iguana came to my attention. Here was a creature that seemed perfect for the job! Seldom given to biting, it can live on a completely vegetarian diet.

Well, this lizard did have a down side as well. That is, if you considered the fact that it could eventually reach six feet long to be a problem. Add to that the fact that an eight-inch baby one cost $49.95 at the time, which was about the cost of four anoles or two geckos.

Which brings up another puzzling fact about the lizard market; why is there such a pattern of rising and declining prices for iguanas? So far the only factor I can find is that when I want to buy one the price is high. When I'm not in the market, they are dirt cheap!

In the end I bought an aquarium to house the critter, a heat lamp to warm it, veggies for its meals and laid out $50 for the lizard itself. It was, however, worth the price to see the pleased look on Zane's birthday when he met his new pet. If I could only end the story right here by saying that everyone lived happily ever after, this would be a warm and fuzzy tale that brings joy to the cockles of one's heart. Unfortunately, there is more to the saga.

Less than a week after the iguana joined the household, it transpired that I was the last one to leave the house on a fateful Thursday morning. This fact was important since I would have no one else upon whom I could place the blame for the ensuing events. Early in the afternoon I swung back by the home place and upon entering the door saw the French doors to the deck were open. Immediately thinking our house had been burgled, I grabbed Zane's baseball bat and began to check the premises for intruders.

To my relief everything seemed in order - until I got to Zane's room. There I made the puzzling discovery that the iguana's aquarium home was empty. Since I had been assured at the pet store that this cage would contain the beasty for a least a couple of years, I was perplexed. Then, I spotted the two eyes of the family yard cat peering up at me from under the bed.

The truth struck like a thunderbolt. Our adopted stray cat came in through the unlatched deck doors and had obviously just finished dining on a $50 lizard! In shear rage I chased the cat through the house with the bat, determined to put an end to the animal. It was, however, too quick for me, bounding out the open deck door and heading from the woods at the back of our yard.

How would Zane take the news when he returned from school to find his birthday present had lasted less than a week and had been eaten by the cat?

There was but one thing to do. I carefully locked up this time, making sure no doors were left ajar. The next stop was at the local pet store to purchase another iguana. If I could get the new lizard into the aquarium before school was out, Zane probably would not even realize anything had happened. Then after a few days I could explain it to him, yet avoid upsetting him about the fate of the first iguana. It seemed like sage, fatherly thinking and the perfect solution to the problem .

With but a few minutes to spare before Zane's

arrival aboard the school bus, I got back from the pet store and placed the new lizard in the aquarium. I was still watching the critter adjust to its new surroundings when Zane entered the room.

"What're you doing, Dad?"

"Just checking out your iguana. He seems to be doing pretty good."

"Yeah, Dad, he's the best pet in the world."

Smugly, I assumed I had pulled it off. But, only for a moment.

"Dad, do iguana's multiply fast?"

"I don't think so," I replied. "Why do you ask?"

"Cause there's another one under the dresser watching us."

To my horror, he was right. Apparently the pet store attendant forgot to mention that iguanas are strong enough jumpers to get out of an aquarium. In a few minutes we had surrounded the loose lizard and added him to our collection in the aquarium. I had never realized how small a $100 collection of lizards really was.

After explaining to Zane what had happened, I next began looking forward to having to tell his mother why I had spent $100 for two reptiles that would some day be six feet long and living in the house with us. The worst part, however, was having to go out in the wood lot to find the cat and apologize to it!

Author's likeness by his son, Zane Jacobs.

About the Author

Outdoorsman and writer Jimmy Jacobs is a life-long resident of Georgia and the award-winning author of four guide books on fishing for trout and bass in the southeastern United States.

With a degree in journalism from Georgia State University in Atlanta, Jacobs turned his love of the outdoors into a career, working for Primedia, Inc. as editor of Georgia Sportsman, Alabama Game & Fish, and Florida Game & Fish magazines. As a free-lancer, his writing has also appeared in more than 20 general interest, travel, entertainment, and outdoor publications.

As an accomplished after-dinner speaker and storyteller, Jacobs is asked to perform at a number of festivals each year and has appeared on local television affiliates in Atlanta and Chattanooga, TN, on Georgia Public Television's nine-station statewide network, SportSouth Cable Network, and WCNN-TV nationally.

His writing and photography have won 18 Excellence in Craft Awards from the Florida Outdoor Writers Association, Georgia Outdoor Writers Association, and the Southeastern Outdoor Press Association.

Other books by Jimmy Jacobs:
Trout Fishing In North Georgia
Trout Streams Of Southern Appalachia
Tailwater Trout In The South
Bass Fishing In Georgia

How To Order
Books by Jimmy Jacobs

	QTY x Price = Extended Price
Moonlight Through The Pines: Tales from Georgia Evenings	$11.95
Bass Fishing in Georgia "...a well-researched, comprehensive guide to public waters,...Jacobs makes it easy to plan a trip..." *Atlanta Journal Constitution*	$13.95
Tailwater Trout In The South Third Place, Excellence in Craft, Best Outdoor Book, Southeastern Outdoor Press Association, 1997	$18.00
Trout Streams of Southern Appalachia "No Dixie trout fisherman should wet a line without reading this invaluable reference first." *Sports Afield*	$17.00
Trout Fishing in North Georgia "Anyone thinking about a trout fishing expedition to North Georgia would be well served by throwing this fine guide in the glove compartment." *Southern Living*	$13.95

Subtotal	
GA Residence, add 5% Sales Tax	
(U.S. Priority Mail) Shipping	$4.00
TOTAL	

Charge It! **By Phone 770-578-9410 or On Line www.franklin-sarrett.com**

☐ Charge my credit card _____
Credit Card Number   Expiration Date

☐ I've enclosed a Money Order or my personal check.

Name_____

Address_____

City/State/Zip_____

——————— MAIL TO ———————

Franklin-Sarrett Publishers • 3761 Vineyard Trace • Marietta, GA 30062